Magical Mayhem

Part Nine

To Prevent Best Friends

Emily Martha Sorensen

Also by Emily Martha Sorensen

Wicked Witches of Restva:
Black Magic Academy
White Magic Academy

The End in the Beginning:
The Keeper and the Rulership
The Fires of the Rulership
The Magic or the Rulership

Fairy Senses:
Fairy Eyeglasses
Fairy Compass
Fairy Earmuffs
Fairy Barometer
Fairy Pox
Fairy Slippers
Fairy Lunchbox
Fairy Icepack
Fairy Stopwatch
Fairy Toothbrush
Fairy Perfume
Fairy Crown

Dragon Eggs:
Dragon's Egg
Dragon's Hope
Dragon's First Christmas
Dragon's Fire
Dragon's Song
Dragon's First Valentine

Comics:
A Magical Roommate
To Prevent World Peace

The Numbers Just Keep
Getting Bigger:
Twenty-Four Potential
Children of Prophecy

Trilogy of a Teenage Werevulture:
Trials of a Teenage Werevulture
Trifles of a Teenage Werevulture

Weredodo Cozy Mysteries:
Weredodo Sleuth

Not Quite a Harem:
Not Quite a Curse

Magical Mayhem:
To Prevent World Peace
To Prevent Chic Costumes
To Prevent Clear Paths
To Prevent Smart Choices
To Prevent Warm Welcomes
To Prevent Cute Mascots
To Prevent First Place (prologue)
To Prevent Fresh Starts
To Prevent New Allies

Short Story Collections:
Worlds of Wonder
Magic and Mischief
Tales of Tie-Ins

Picture Books:
Tabby, Tabby, Burning Bright

To Prevent Best Friends

http://www.emilymarthasorensen.com

To Frederik Vendelin,

longtime fan of the comic,
reader of my other books,
and Patreon supporter.

Chapter 1
The Surveillance

Rhea was hard at work, furiously trying to make sense of the egregious nonsense her predecessor had left behind. It seemed Great-Uncle Nico's idiocy about foreign policy had been equaled only by his incompetence at domestic management.

She heard a rustle from behind her. Annoyed, she flicked a quick glance at her arm to check a split second into the past, saw it was Minerva standing there, and didn't bother to turn around.

"Ma'am?" her minion ventured from the doorway. "The peons are complaining again."

"Let them," Rhea snorted derisively. "They're all too afraid of me to do anything about it."

"I . . . I don't think they are. They're saying things like 'lazy' and 'weak' . . ."

"*Lazy?*" Rhea exploded, looking over her shoulder. "Do they have any idea what a *mess* Great-Uncle Nico left me?!"

"No, but I don't think they c—"

"His records on renegade family members are ridiculously sloppy," Rhea fumed. "He hadn't updated the file on Chronos in over a decade, the file about me misspelled the name of my store, and did you know that I have a third cousin twice removed with grandchildren currently living in Argos who don't even know they're Olympians?!"

"Boss, I don't think the peons are intere—"

"And mismanagement of *funds!*" Rhea exclaimed. "He hadn't paid a minion or assassin in years, which means all the competent ones quit years ago. The only ones who stayed were either family or terrified of him, which left a pathetic selection. And do you know how many infiltrators he had among our rivals and enemies? Do you? Do you?"

Minerva was suppressing a yawn. "N—" she began.

"ZERO!" Rhea screamed, clenching her fists. "That complete idiot!"

Minerva sighed. "I didn't say I agreed with them, boss. I just said that the idiots are getting restless. Why don't you just blackmail somebody to keep them happy?"

Rhea turned and gave her minion a flat stare.

Minerva folded her arms, not remotely cowed.

In the silence, Rhea's gaze flitted across her minion's outfit, evaluating the skill with which it had been put together. She had to admit, it was pretty clever.

Minerva wore two ponytails, one at the top left side and one at the bottom right, which made her look off-balance and potentially out of her mind. The skirt she wore was slashed up to the hip in twelve places, allowing her arrowhead tail free range of movement, as well showing off enough of her legs to be highly distracting to any men who came near. And the starburst necklace she wore was a subtle, yet terrifying, threat.

To most people, of course, it would seem no more than a pretty piece of jewelry. It was the sort of accessory Rhea might have given to a magical girl. But for the Olympian minions who had spent decades placating a man with the power to kill people with an explosion of power that took that exact shape . . . well . . .

Approval at her minion's choice of fashion softened Rhea's irritability somewhat.

"Simple-minded cretins . . ." Rhea muttered. Why was blackmail the only thing her family ever thought she was capable of doing? Still, there was no doubt that she was brilliant at it. "Fine. I'll check up on that goody-goody president of Mágico."

As she spoke, she raised her hand. It wasn't strictly necessary for checking the past, but it made it easier to focus if she made some sort of physical, symbolic gesture.

"I've never managed to find anything in her squeaky clean past before," Rhea mused, staring at her hand as her mind flashed through a series of press conferences, "but it's been a few months since I've bothered to look. Perhaps she's finally done something actually worth . . ." Images flickered across her mind. ". . . what . . ."

She stopped abruptly.

". . . IS THIS?!" Rhea finished in a wild scream, staring at her fists incredulously.

"Got no idea . . ." Minerva murmured, not even bothering to hide a yawn this time.

Rhea stared in horror at her fists without seeing them, the images racing in a jumble of ghastliness across her mind. The situation was even worse than she'd suspected from that first glimpse.

"Who in their right mind would start a Magical Girl Union?!" Rhea exploded, leaping to her feet. "They're much too powerful already!!"

"Whoa." Minerva's yawn slapped shut, and she looked stunned. "I've never even heard of . . ."

"Of course you haven't," Rhea muttered, staring slightlessly off to the side. All she could see was more, more, more of those terrible plans unfurling in a distant country. "It's not officially launched yet. They haven't announced it; all the plans are still currently confidential. They've only been planning three months. But *three months* — in which I didn't notice it?!"

"Er . . ." Minerva looked uncomfortable. "Well, you've been busy . . ."

"That is absolutely no excuse." Rhea covered her face with her fists, buried in humiliation. "I should never, *ever* fail to catch important information. If I had caught this three months ago, I could have nipped it in the bud. Now, it's had enough time to grow that it could become a real threat."

"Do you really think so?" Minerva asked worriedly.

Rhea didn't raise her head. The further back she dove, the more it spiraled to become worse and worse. There was *competence* in those enemies, and she had no one competent except Minerva to work with here.

"How about assassination?" Minerva asked hopefully.

"With whom?" Rhea demanded, raising her head. "I can't call a freelance assassin because they're all boycotting Olympus Estates for not having paid them. I can't send a family member because none of the ones who stuck around for Great-Uncle Nico are a remotely close match for the girls involved in the Union. And even if that weren't the case, the last thing we want is to give those girls a martyr!"

Minerva swallowed. "Is it really that bad?"

"Worse," Rhea said grimly. "Do you have any idea how much work it's going to take to undo this?!"

Minerva shook her head, uneven ponytails flapping.

Rhea looked down and clutched the top of her head and recited:

"They've already recruited Tat'yana Tsvetok . . . Golden Tingle Spray . . . Schönwasser . . . Dulcina Caramelo . . . Namikaze Tateru . . . Chung-Ae . . . La Rama Fragrante . . . Xinghuo . . . Snowbelle . . . Delicate Frost Princess . . . Météore . . . Some former Pink Dragon is running the thing . . ."

Rhea's hands dropped from her head in crashing realization. "WAIT A MINUTE!"

"What?" Minerva asked, alarmed.

"Pink Dragon!" Rhea shouted. "Pink Dragon!"

"Who's —"

Rhea checked back in the past of that girl, and sure enough, she saw a familiar scene.

There was Kendra, speaking vehemently to a brown-skinned girl wearing the same fluffy pink dress that was now being put in all the Magical Girl Union marketing materials. Kendra was saying, *"I became a villain for the same reason we both became magical girls: to protect world peace!"*

Rhea slammed her fist on the desk. She'd never been more angry.

"Who . . .?" Minerva ventured, looking nervous.

"Cream Angel's best friend," Rhea said grimly. "Oh, my sister had *better* not be behind this."

Chapter 2
The Concealment

In a lair not all that distant from Olympus Estates, tucked away on an island close to the coast of Greece, Rhea's sister was staring at a chart of magical girl team symbols, trying to remember which one she was supposed to cross off next.

It's not enough for me to tell her what I see, oh no, Chronos thought grumpily. *Now Kendra wants me to keep track of all my visions on an organized chart. Exactly how am I supposed to remember which team symbol is which?*

Yes, okay, so technically, Chronos could simply check the futures that all those symbols appeared in. But it wasn't like all of them were unique. Greased Lightning, for instance, had almost the same symbol on the headband of her new magical girl form as the three lightning bolts that were supposed to signify The Spazzes, a trio of magical girl sisters who kept using their electrical powers to play pranks on their teachers.

Granted, the chart before this one had been filled with names instead of symbols, and that had been even worse. After the third time Chronos had accidentally sent Kendra after a magical girl with the same name as the one she was actually supposed to stop, Kendra had torn down the old chart and stapled up the one with symbols instead.

But Chronos didn't see why the new chart couldn't have had both names *and* symbols.

Or better yet, they could go back to no chart at all.

Was this one . . . Fusion Girl? Chronos wondered, her hand with the pen wavering as she stared at the chart. *Or was that cluster of three circles with the fire around it Triple Sunbeams?*

She didn't even remember what her second dream had been about anymore.

Chronos decided to give up on that particular symbol. If it was important, she'd dream about it again, whether she liked it or not. She glanced at another symbol with a snoozing wolf and "LW" in fancy script next to it. *Oh, right. Lone Wolf is probably going to join the Dingo Darlings. Uh . . . is there even space on this chart to draw a new symbol on?*

The sound of footsteps headed into the plotting room.

Recognizing the cocky stride, Chronos didn't bother to turn around. "Welcome back, Kendra."

"Yup. How'd the future change?"

Chronos glanced at her left hand, the one holding the pen. She saw no difference in the future of the translator Kendra had hired, and the sandstorm hitting the city was now in ninety-eight percent of the futures, rather than sixty percent. That seemed a bit odd, but perhaps the weather patterns had changed. Thankfully, there were no longer any futures with a magical girl snapping and making it much worse.

"The storm's still going to happen, but there's not much you can do about the weather," Chronos surmised. "It looks like you convinced Farah to stop stalking her ex-boyfriend. She's not going to freak out when he goes on that date with her sister and destroy the city. How was Dubai?"

"Long. Hot. And sandy." There was a *thump*.

Chronos turned around and glanced behind her. Kendra had casually hopped up onto the table and was sitting on it. She removed one of her boots and shook it upside down, making a face.

"I *did* send you after a magical girl with sandstorm powers," Chronos said, shrugging. "Sand is to be expected."

"Yes, and believe me, she made use of it." The cocksure blonde fifteen-year-old rolled her eyes. "At least she won't be able to do *that* anymore. Y'know, I think there's even sand in my underwear. That might be my new least favorite power. Good riddance to it."

Alarmed, Chronos scanned the future for Farah's magical girl form, Halimah. It was, fortunately, still there. But in all of them, her outfit was changed, and she no longer wore the necklace that had been the centerpiece of it. She also seemed to have different powers and poor control over them, the sort of thing you would expect from a new magical girl, rather than an experienced one.

"You broke her focus item, didn't you?" Chronos accused.

Kendra shrugged. "I'm sure she'll make another one."

"That necklace belonged to her mother! It was an heirloom focus item! The extra powers it had can't be replaced!"

"Then she should've stopped sending sandstorms my way and should've listened to me."

Chronos breathed in deeply, trying to keep her temper in check. Yes, breaking the girl's focus item was one way to guarantee she wouldn't be able to cause mass devastation. But it was *also* a way to guarantee that the girl wouldn't be around to redirect the storm when it hit a month from now, if she was feeling more sane.

This explained why there was now a much higher chance that the storm would hit the city and cause mild destruction.

"Do you understand the concept of 'only as a last resort'?!" Chronos snarled. "I told you to talk some sense into her!"

"I tried. She didn't want to talk. She attacked the translator as well as me. I fixed the problem." Kendra shrugged.

Chronos's jaw clenched.

Yes, the magical girl's tantrum over finding out her ex-boyfriend was in love with her sister would've resulted in the worst sandstorm Dubai had dealt with in twenty years.

Yes, in most futures, she would have gotten off scot free with no one realizing she'd been responsible for making it worse, and in a few futures, an innocent born mage with wind powers would have been blamed for causing the storm instead.

Yes, she had sent Kendra to prevent those possibilities.

But Chronos had specifically said to *"leave the villain costume behind."* She also distinctly remembered emphasizing the phrase *"by nonviolent means."*

She had not, at any point, said, *"You know what would be a really good idea? You could show up as a villain, provoke her into attacking you, and break her focus item!"*

"Well, thank you for doing something to stop the sandstorm, even though it wasn't what I asked you to do, it got rid of all the best futures as well as all the worst ones, and you could have done it in a much better way," Chronos said sarcastically.

"You're welcome," Kendra answered. "When are you going to send me after the Magical Girl Union already?"

Chronos stared at her incredulously. *When am I going to . . .? When you just barely chose a violent solution over the superior one I asked you to use?*

"Stop asking me that," Chronos said with exasperation. "Their future is still in flux. At least three-quarters of their futures are neutral or decent. I'll send you only *when* their future's settled, and *if* it proves necessary."

"*IF?!*" Kendra exploded, flinging her arms out wide. "This is the Magical Girl Union we're talking about! This is the organization I would have founded to take over the world! I have to destroy them! *TELL ME WHERE IT IS!*"

Funnily enough, this display of coolheaded rationality did not budge Chronos.

Given who's involved in it, and your propensity to overreact . . .? Not likely.

"No," Chronos said, turning around. She could feel a vicious and intense glare burning holes in her back, but she ignored that and went back to making notes on the board.

She scribbled out the logo for Collective Lightning, a team that Greased Lightning might have founded, because all her futures now contained a new mascot that had been assigned to her from the Australian Mascot Bureau instead.

This one was, fortunately, not a criminal from another world, which made for a welcome change.

Also, Rainbow Fusion and Bright as Gold had apparently not met on the bus during the day it had been likely they would, given that there were no longer any futures with the two being friends, which meant both falling in love with the same boy and fighting over him wasn't likely to happen, so she crossed those logos out.

There was an irritated clearing of throat behind her.

"No," Chronos said indifferently. "You can stare at me as long as you want. I don't care."

There was a sliding sound. She glanced back to see Kendra no longer on the table, now heading out of the room. "You can't keep this from me forever, *soothsayer.* I'm starting to think you don't trust me."

"I don't," Chronos said flatly. "Remember Chinchilla Fluffhair?"

Kendra gave an exaggerated sigh. "How was I supposed to know the girl would dive in front of my halo to save her teammate? Good grief."

"I told you she had three futures in which she would do that with other villains! I told you that she hero-worshiped that girl! I told you to attack when she wasn't there!"

"And how was I supposed to know that was relevant?"

"YOU COULD HAVE LISTENED TO ME!!"

Kendra headed out of the room, blithely ignoring this.

"Hey, Tiff!" her voice came from the other room. "Next target's an easy one! Want to come with me?"

Tiffany's voice squealed. "Ooh, yay! I'll bring Maisie!"

"No mask."

"But I need —"

"NO MASK."

"Maisie's gonna be all lonelyyyyyyyyyy!"

Chronos quickly checked her hands to make sure Kendra's next target was one that couldn't be botched easily. Fortunately, Kendra was right; a magical girl thief without any combat powers was exactly the kind of mission that would be perfect to train the ten-year-old in. That was a good judgment call.

Granted, Kendra could have bothered to ask her boss first, which she never quite seemed to do, but whatever.

The Concealment

Being part of a team hadn't been Chronos's first choice, or for that matter her second or third or fourth, but if she had to be in one, she was glad to see the other members getting along.

This was especially true because, for a long time, Kendra had treated the ten-year-old with sneering derision. Chronos wasn't very good at reading other people's feelings, but Tiffany's sobfests about always being left behind had made it pretty obvious how she felt about not being treated as an equal teammate.

But the last few months, things had been better. Ever since Tiffany had proven herself useful on their first mission together, Kendra had started inviting her along on simple missions. Not only did that make Tiffany happy, it meant that Chronos got some peace and quiet to herself occasionally.

Chronos flicked through the magical girl thief's futures, looking for a selection of scenes to show them so they'd know what kind of powers the girl had. As she chose some representative moments, she also tossed in a few that showed the girl's ideology so that they'd know why she was trying to rob her current target instead of the little things she usually did.

"Look! Now Maisie has a disguise! I can wear her!"

"You cannot wear a mask on top of another mask!"

Chronos picked a few scenes that showed why the thief was popular with children in the city, just in case that was relevant, and then headed out of the room to debrief her subordinates who occasionally paid attention to the advice she gave them.

She had a vague, nagging feeling that she might have forgotten something, but a quick glance at the general futures of the world showed nothing important about to happen, so she pushed the thought away.

"Ugh . . ."

Florence dropped the thick biology textbook on the floor and flopped back across her bed, spreading her arms.

"Too . . . much . . . work . . ." she groaned.

It wasn't just her homework, though that was part of it.

The real problem was that tomorrow was the day the official announcement would be made about the Magical Girl Union, and once that came out, she would be a worldwide figure. A celebrity.

Yesterday had been a typical Thursday at school, except for the fact that she'd gone in to talk to the principal about the possibility of taking the rest of this year's classes by correspondence, with the vague excuse of "I might be going out of town for awhile."

The principal, who like everyone else in town knew that blabbermouth Felicity's secret identity and suspected Florence was her former teammate, had winked at her knowingly and started setting up a schedule, no doubt assuming that Pink Dragon was planning to go to a different world to save a mascot civilization or something.

The fact that he wasn't far off made it even more frustrating.

Florence preferred privacy; she was the one who'd insisted on secret identities in the first place. And now her face would be debuting on the front page of newspapers all over the world.

Kendra would have loved it. Florence hated it. But she had to accept it to run the Magical Girl Union.

Florence leaned over to pick up the textbook and tried to go back to reading it, but her stomach was fluttering, and she couldn't concentrate on the passage she was supposed to be reading and answering questions about. Now that she was thinking about the Magical Girl Union, it was all she could think about.

Two weeks from now was the official launch. And it was going to be huge. All the girls on the board of directors would be giving a speech, and then Edelweiss, a popular singing magical girl, would perform a free concert.

They'd tried to get Lentswe Counterpoint, but she refused to perform live outside of South Africa, to Florence's disappointment and Snowbelle's loud protests.

In any case, that day was coming up soon.

In some ways, it felt like the planning had taken forever. They'd been putting things together, meeting every two weeks, for three months now. In other ways, it felt like time had zoomed past, and the yawning chasm of pressure was now right in front of her.

The Concealment

She was grateful that they'd kept it confidential for as long as they had, and rather amazed that they'd managed it. Dulcina had made the point in their first meeting with Presidente Santos that if they held a press conference at the beginning, it would give villains and hostile governments a chance to prepare to counter their influence before they could put it in place.

So, even knowing it wouldn't last much longer, Florence had been able to keep pretending her life was normal. She'd done her homework, attended track practice, gone to church, and only worked on the Magical Girl Union in private, filling every spare moment with preparations.

The downside of that was that she was swamped beyond belief, leaving her no time to ponder her new magical girl form. Between choosing which tasks to assign to which members of the board, breaking up inevitable squabbles, keeping track of the finances, trying to get through the enormous book of Mágico laws for magical girls, sweating over her speech, occasionally trying to pick up a few words of Portuguese . . .

A tentative knock came on her door. It opened, and her little brother poked his head through. "Flo? You promised we could play an hour ago . . ."

"Ack!" Florence sat bolt upright. "I forgot about that! I — I don't know if I can, Jacob. I still have three tons of homework, plus that humongous book Presidente Santos gave me . . ."

"Florence," her mother said firmly, stepping in after Jacob. She must have been doing the dishes, because she was drying a dripping wet glass with a cloth. "Your brother's more important than your homework. *Go. Play.*"

Ashamed that she'd been trying to weasel out of her word, Florence nodded. She dropped the book and headed outside with her brother, who was excitedly tossing the basketball in the air and jabbering about how much better his jump shot had gotten and how he was going to crush her to smithereens.

Once they started playing, some of her worries faded a bit. She loved basketball, and had been on the team for a year before she'd decided to switch to track instead.

Jacob *had* gotten better. They were evenly matched now. Either that, or she'd gotten worse because her head wasn't completely in the game. Whatever the reason, he was more fun to play against than he used to be, and chasing after her brother and blocking his shots soothed some of her mind's frantic, spiraling pace.

She couldn't get her mind to stop entirely, though.

Two weeks. Just two weeks.

Florence dribbled the ball, and Jacob dodged to try to grab it. She shot to the side and leapt for a basket. The ball bounced off the back.

What was I thinking when I volunteered to do this? Running an international government? Was I insane?

Jacob snatched the ball and ran off with it, dribbling rapidly.

Florence tried to grab it, but he feinted left, then right, then left, then shot, and — basket!

I'm about to spend the entire summer in Mágico. I may even need to move there permanently.

That was why she'd promised to spend time with Jacob now. It might be one of their last chances to play together.

Florence leapt in the air and blocked a shot from her brother. Then she caught the ball and raced across the court, dribbling. She shot and — the ball went in! Yes!

"Two-two!" Jacob grinned, slapping her five. "But I'll win."

Florence laughed. "Not happening, squirt!"

As she ran across the court, Jacob stole the ball from her and launched into the air. His shot bounced off the rim and landed straight in one of Mom's rosebushes.

Jacob groaned and ran over there to retrieve it.

Florence watched him gingerly poking his fingers through the thorns, trying to reach it, and wondered with a sharp pang of regret how much she was going to see him in the future.

Everyone treats me like I have some idea what I'm doing. Florence watched her brother wince and yank his hand back, glaring at the thorny plant. *But I don't! All I have is a little last-minute research and a wild-eyed dream!*

Anyone would have been more qualified than her.

But she was the one who'd volunteered to do it.

Jacob was back on the driveway, grinning. He raced towards the basket, dribbling tightly. Florence ran in and stole the ball, arcing away from him. Jacob ducked under her arm and stole the ball back, jumping up to throw it at the basket.

"Score!" he yelled. "Two-three!"

"Watch me get my revenge!" Florence yelled, determined to pay more attention and play better.

But her brain wouldn't cooperate and shut down.

All of the sixteen magical girls we've recruited now are more powerful than I'll ever be. So why does anyone think I know what I'm doing? Why would anyone entrust this to me?

She ran towards the basket, dribbling, and threw. The ball bounced off the rim.

"HA!" Jacob shouted. "Some revenge! Still two-three!"

She tried to grab the ball, but Jacob reached it first and leapt in the air, crowing wildly. The ball went in.

Florence gave herself a brief sigh. She wasn't even that good at the things she was actually good at.

Seriously, what was I thinking when I volunteered to do this? Was I insane?

From the doorway, Ellen and John were watching their children race across the driveway, battling over the basketball.

"What were we thinking when we volunteered to let her do this?" Ellen asked quietly. "Were we insane?"

Her husband put his arm around her waist. He didn't ask what she meant. "You know what we said three months ago."

"I know. I know she's old enough to make her own decisions, but . . . isn't she way too young to do something like *this?* We're talking about a major political position. We're talking about her being a public figure with no personal life. We're talking about her dropping out of school and never finishing it."

John nodded. They both knew that Florence's optimistic plans to finish school by correspondence weren't particularly realistic.

They hadn't said anything to her because . . . well, it was always possible that they might be wrong. She could surprise them. And there was no reason to discourage her from trying.

But they were both expecting that their sixteen-year-old daughter would soon decide that it wasn't possible to finish school and continue her career track, and she'd drop the one that was least important. The choice she would make at that point was inevitable, and they could hardly begrudge it.

But they could worry. They could definitely worry.

"It's a lot better than what Olivia and Richard are going through," John said quietly. "She included us in her decision. She invited us to help her. She even asked our permission."

Ellen nodded, a lump in her throat. It was much, much better to have a daughter who was going into politics to make a positive difference to the world this young than it was to have a daughter who defected to villainy.

Ellen and Olivia had been friends for almost as long as Florence and Kendra had been best friends, a natural consequence of their having two young daughters who wanted to spend all their time together.

While their daughters had grown apart over time, Olivia and Ellen hadn't. They had different views and opinions, perhaps, and extremely different taste in husbands, but neither of them found it hard to respect the other.

When Kendra had defected to villainy and left her parents behind, without even so much as an explanation, Richard had taken the news at first grimly and then with humor, while Olivia had settled into a deep depression. She'd needed a lot of friendship to climb out of it.

So Ellen knew, far better than most, how much they had to be grateful for. Florence was staying on the side of justice, following the law, honoring her parents, and simply forging a difficult path that nobody else had done before.

"Besides." John put his hand on her shoulder. "She was old enough to help the FBI out when she was twelve. Remember what we said then?"

Ellen nodded, with difficulty. "If it's God's will that she be safe . . . then she will be. If it isn't . . . then that's His decision."

John nodded. "This isn't so different. We both felt peace when we prayed about it. This is even far less dangerous than that was. Think of it like college . . . or a foreign exchange."

"But she's only *sixteen!*" Ellen whispered.

She knew she was being irrational, but it still made her fret.

"And I'm sure she'll be fine." Her husband embraced her. "Have faith."

Chapter 3
The Revelation

Moving stealthily, a magical girl climbed up a wall behind one of the pillars of the British Museum, a safety rope attached to her left ankle in case she happened to stumble and fall.

An eleven-year-old cat burglar couldn't be too careful, after all, especially since no one could see her unless they already knew she was there. If she fell and hurt herself, no one would know they should call an ambulance.

Her fingers grasped a handhold, and she pulled herself a few more inches up.

The idea of flight powers had never occurred to her, because thieves didn't fly; they climbed. She thought wings looked silly on people, anyway. But now she wondered if she should have considered a power like magically jumping, or something.

Maybe she would do that if she powered up at some point. Would she power up tonight? It was her first major heist, after all!

So far, most of her thefts had been things like stealing the teacher's test answers and posting them in the hallway so that everyone's grades could be equal, stealing the trophies out of the sports case so that nobody could be better than anyone else, and stealing one of Mrs. Ellis's wigs to give to Mr. Adam because he was balding and didn't have one.

The Revelation

For some reason, neither of them had ever thanked the local magical girl thief for that.

But she was a heroine with the other schoolchildren here in London. They often left notes for her by the statue of Edward VIII, the king she most admired because it was during his reign in the ancient 1950s that England had become a socialist state.

They would ask her to steal back their money from bullies, or to steal their father away from work so that he'd come to a game they were playing in, or to steal them candy from a store that unfairly wanted them to pay money for it.

And of course Alice always obliged. She believed in equality for all. She had magic and they didn't, which meant she had to use her magic for the good of everybody. It was the only way things would be fair.

Sometimes the police would take those notes from beneath that statue, so she'd have to sneak into the police station to steal her notes back. That was often tricky when they had magical girl aides present, especially Alice's twelve-year-old rival who fancied herself a detective, but Alice always outwitted them and collected her notes. She was clever and sneaky.

This, though . . . this was a new thing. She had never robbed a museum before. She was nervous.

She'd watched TV to prepare for it, and she'd done everything the way you were supposed to. She'd sent a note to the curator to tell him what she was going to be stealing, she'd sent another one to her rival, and she'd sent a third one to the newspaper, because she knew it would be really exciting to see her magical girl name as a headline the next morning.

Now all she had to do was succeed.

Her heart pounded with excitement as she climbed the next few inches of the pillar.

Soon enough, she'd have the Rosetta Stone in her possession, and she'd send it back to Egypt, where it belonged. Everyone would praise her as the heroine who'd righted an old injustice, the police would be befuddled, and maybe she would do it again with something else that needed to be returned.

She had just barely learned in school that there were lots and lots of things in the British Museum that had been stolen from other countries that wanted them back. She didn't know what the rest were yet, but she would learn what they were, and then she would —

She felt a tug at her ankle, and then suddenly she was jerked from the wall and swinging through open air. *"WAH!"*

"Seriously?" a sardonic voice said above her. "Who *leaves notes* saying what they're going to be stealing?"

Alice gasped in panic. Was it a new magical girl detective? That wasn't her rival's voice. How had the person above known where she was? It was impossible to find her unless you knew exactly where to look!

No, no, no, no. That didn't matter. What mattered right now was escaping.

"You can't hold me!" Alice declared. "I am . . ."

She whipped through a spin like a frantic yo-yo, whipping out of the leg cuff and exploding into full visibility. A brilliant red cloak appeared behind her, and she struck a dramatic pose.

". . . Robbin' Red Riding Hood! I steal from the rich to feed the poor!"

A squeal and clapping came from above. Alice looked up to see a girl with yellow corkscrew pigtails. "Wow! That's so cool! I knew you'd be amazing!"

The detective beside her, who seemed to be wearing black, didn't look impressed.

"You live in *Marxist England,*" she said in an American accent. "*What* rich? *What* poor? Who's supposed to be Prince John in your story?"

Alice flipped her hood over her head and glowered. "What right do you have to question me?"

"Not to mention that you're robbing a *museum,* which isn't going to feed anybody . . ."

"So cool! So cool! I knew you would be!" the girl with pigtails squealed, jumping up and down. "That's why I sent the police on a wild goose chase away from here!"

The Revelation

"WHAT?!" the detective girl roared, turning to face her.

Alice took this as her cue to bolt into the darkness.

"Tiffany," Kendra said in a flat voice, glowering at her worse-than-useless teammate. "I'm going to kill you."

"You only said to *get* the police," the moron said with huge, innocent eyes. "You didn't tell me *where* to send them . . ."

Kendra made a mental note to teleport Tiffany up to the roof of the lair and leave her there for several hours after they got back home. Then she looked down at their quarry.

No sign of the thief.

"And now you've let her *escape!*" Kendra shouted.

"Yaaaaaaaaaaaaaaaaaay!"

There was a glimpse of red down below. It seemed the thief had forgotten to make her always-visible cloak disappear before activating her stealth power. What an idiot.

Kendra teleported into the path of the magical girl thief.

"Going somewhere?" she demanded, readying her halo.

Boxes selling newspapers exploded on both sides of the alley, knocking Kendra off her feet and burying her in them.

"Apparently so," she muttered, shoving the bundles of paper away and looking around.

There was no longer any sign of Robbin' Red Riding Hood. Apparently she wasn't as stupid as she'd seemed. The visible cloak must have been meant to lure Kendra into a trap.

The thief was gone. And Kendra couldn't count on the police to help out, because her beyond-worthless teammate had done something to lure them away.

In other words, this mission was a complete catastrophe.

I'll have to check with Chronos to see if she's going to come back to the museum tonight, Kendra thought, irate. *If not, we'll finish this on whatever day she does.*

"Wait up for me!" Tiffany shouted, running down the street. She stopped, seeing the pile of newspapers. "Wow, that's a lot!"

"I noticed," Kendra said grumpily.

"Where do we find her next?" Tiffany asked eagerly.

Kendra glowered at the pigtailed girl. "You mean, so you can help her instead of me?"

"Uh huh!"

Kendra grabbed a newspaper, rolled it up, and whacked the side of her teammate's head.

"Owwww!" Tiffany complained.

A bit of the bold headline in her hand caught Kendra's eye.

Magica

She unrolled it, and her breath caught tight in her throat. The headline at the very top of the first page said:

Magical Girl Union

And off to the right was a picture.

A picture of a very stiff girl with brown skin and black braids, wearing a cross necklace, trying to force a smile.

It was Florence.

There was no doubt it was Florence.

She looked exactly that way in every school picture she'd ever posed for.

Her fingers clenching so hard that the paper tore under them, Kendra looked down at the caption. It seemed tailor-made to remove any doubt:

Florence Atkins: Future Leader of the Union?

The newspaper slipped from Kendra's hands. She stood there, frozen in disbelief.

Leader of the Union.

LEADER OF THE UNION.

Florence is the leader of the Magical Girl Union?!

No. No, that wasn't possible.

That wasn't possible, right?

Of course she'd assumed that the oracle was hiding something. She'd assumed that meant that the girl building the Union was someone she admired, such as Namikaze Tateru, Chung-Ae, or Dulcina Caramelo.

She'd never considered the possibility of Florence.

Florence, her best friend.

Florence, the one with the ridiculous overactive conscience.

Florence . . . who had been in the Magical Girl Union in that nightmare future as one of Kendra's chief henchwomen.

Kendra swallowed. Her mouth was dry, and her stomach felt queasy. A memory from a few months before she'd met Chronos swam through her mind.

"You know what the world really needs?" her idiot past self had told her teammates, shortly before they'd killed Queen Hemlock and right after she'd read the first draft of her mom's biography of Chung-Ae. *"An organization to stand up for magical girl rights. Like the Righteous Army in Korea."*

"Or we could just base the whole government around them, like Mágico or Moon Base," Florence had laughed. *"That wouldn't cause any problems."*

"It wouldn't!" Kendra had said indignantly. *"Moon Base and Mágico are awesome!"*

Florence had seemed to think Kendra was joking, despite her having been perfectly serious. But maybe . . . maybe Florence had taken it more seriously than she'd realized.

Maybe Florence had remembered that whole conversation.

Maybe Florence had thought it was a good idea, too.

Kendra leaned over, seized the newspaper she'd held, and ripped it in half.

Why did she have to choose THIS as the first thing she's ever listened to me about?!

Tiffany interrupted her thoughts by grabbing her arm.

"Can we steal things from the museum ourselves?" the idiot little girl asked excitedly. "We're villains, right? That's okay when you're a villain!"

"You! Stay!" Kendra snapped. "Don't go anywhere, don't do anything, unless it's to help the cops catch the thief!"

"But I don't want t—"

Kendra was already teleporting back to the lair.

She landed on the inside of the entrance so that she could storm down the stairs at as high a volume as possible.

Stomp stomp stomp stomp stomp stomp stomp stomp stomp "CHRONOS!"

So much for her peace and quiet. The lair without either Kendra or Tiffany had been nice while it lasted.

Chronos didn't bother to look up from her crocheting. She flicked through her mind to figure out the source of Kendra's ire. It was easy to guess what it was: the magical girl thief had very few futures in jail, which meant she must have escaped.

"If you're looking for Robbin' Red Riding Hood, she'll be back at the museum in ten minutes," Chronos announced, moving her hook into a loop on her left finger. "She seems to have decided to steal the Elgin Marbles instead and send them to Egypt, never mind that that's not where the Elgin Marbles are from. I suggest you stop her."

Kendra stormed across the room and held a newspaper in front of her accusingly, radiating silent fury.

Chronos flicked through the future and figured out why.

"I presume she lured you into an alley with newspaper boxes, which exploded and buried you." Chronos accidentally dropped a loop and ignored it. It was too much bother to fix, and a few dropped loops wouldn't make that much difference. "She's going to be using that maneuver later tonight when the police are chasing her, and she'll probably get away. Now go stop her before she tries to return those artifacts to Egypt and makes Greece really upset and causes an international incident."

Kendra shoved the newspaper in front of Chronos's face and jabbed her finger at the picture right next to the headline. "You want to see an international incident? Look at *THIS!!*"

Chronos blinked and looked at it more closely. She registered the picture for the first time. She had seen the future of it being printed the night before last.

"Oh, *that* newspaper . . ." she hedged.

"FLORENCE!" Kendra shouted.

"Ummmmm . . ."

"IT'S FLORENCE!"

"It does look like it might be . . ."

"YOU KNEW ALL ALONG IT WAS FLORENCE!"

"About that —"

"WHY IS FLORENCE INVOLVED IN THE UNION?!"

Chronos pushed the paper out of her face, getting irritated. "If you read the caption, I'm sure you'll figure that out."

"FUTURE! LEADER!" Kendra shouted, jabbing her finger at it. "FLORENCE!"

Chronos sighed and rubbed her forehead. "Look, I couldn't see how you might react if I told you. I figured you might fly off the handle, and it looks like you did. Like I told you, the future of the Magical Girl Union isn't settled yet. It might even become a good thing. So why don't you just leave her alone? I know you two don't want to be enemies . . ."

"Enemies?" The former magical girl stared at her as if she'd just said something nonsensical. "Are you *crazy?*"

"Uh . . ." Chronos stared at her. "Isn't she?"

"Of course not. She's my best friend." Kendra looked disgusted. "Obviously."

"So . . . you're not out to destroy the Magical Girl Union?"

"Of course I'm going to destroy it!" Kendra yelled.

"So . . . Florence *is* your enemy?"

"NO!"

"You do understand that they're on the same side, right?"

Kendra gave her a contemptuous look. "Florence is my best friend. You're just a teammate. *Her* enemy? I'd sooner be *yours*. You *idiot!*"

Then she teleported out without a single added word.

Chronos stared at the place she had been, speechless.

What . . . in the world . . . did that mean?

Was she defecting to the Magical Girl Union?

Was she planning to kill Florence to save her from herself?

Was she planning to kill *Chronos* for not telling her sooner?

Chronos started to sweat. She had no clue what the former magical girl was thinking, and that scared her. She wasn't very good at predicting behavior without her power even at the best of times, and Kendra was the most volatile person she'd ever met. Chronos had pretty much never successfully guessed what she would do.

And this is why I really, really wish I could see futures I'm involved in. Chronos put her face in her hands. *Blast Kendra for being so utterly unpredictable . . .*

Chapter 4
The Confrontation

Breathing in a regretful sigh, Florence paused at the front door of the school. It was early Friday morning, and rather than going to class like she usually would, she had just cleared out her locker and was heading out the front door.

The halls were empty right now because everyone else was in their first period class. She'd timed it that way on purpose. The news would be spreading by now, and she wanted to slip in and out with nobody the wiser.

If she'd been smart, she would have cleared it out yesterday, but she hadn't thought of it. There were so many things on her mind that she felt scatterbrained nowadays. Then again, maybe it was for the best. It gave her one last chance to look around at her school.

Florence looked nostalgically at the ceiling, where Felicity had once accidentally grown tulips, and Kendra had needed to transform and use her power to erase short-term memories on everyone who had seen Felicity use magic in front of them.

She glanced back at the principal's office, where Kendra had once spent quality time because she hadn't turned in homework for three weeks, because she'd been too busy coming up with strategies to beat Dark Deathwave.

She glanced down the hallway towards the lunchroom, where she and Kendra had so often argued about whether they should go back to being police aides.

Life had been so simple back then.

Stressful, but simple.

Annoying, but simple.

Complicated, but simple.

Okay, fine, life had been a real pain back then, but Florence missed it anyway.

Mostly, she missed her best friend. She missed Kendra badly. But part of her missed Felicity, too.

Felicity was still here in school, but they had nothing in common anymore. She'd always been the odd girl out, really only part of their friendship group because they were on the same magical girl team. So now that Felicity's magic was gone, it was only natural that she'd gravitated toward a new group of friends.

That was fine. It was. It really was. It was just that . . . it hurt to be the one that was outgrown and left behind.

Especially after Kendra's betrayal.

She felt a pang for what she had lost. For the years that she and Kendra and Felicity had spent together. For the comfortable old relationships that now were gone.

For the normal life she would have lived if only Kendra hadn't betrayed them.

She stood there staring at the front doors, reluctant to walk out. Once she did, that meant it was over. Once she did, that meant she had officially moved from her familiar old life into the terrifying unknown. She knew she had to do it, but . . . but . . .

"Florence!" a voice shouted from behind her, and footsteps came pounding.

Florence jerked out of her thoughts and turned around. There was Felicity, running towards her.

"Uh . . . hi," she said awkwardly.

"What's this I hear about you *quitting school?*" Felicity exclaimed, reaching her position and leaning forward in horror. "Mrs. Layton said you won't be in class anymore!"

The Confrontation

Florence winced. It hadn't occurred to her that anyone would show up to confront her right while she was leaving.

"I'm not quitting," she said quickly. "I'm finishing the rest by correspondence. I've worked out a schedule."

"That isn't the same at all!" Felicity cried, flinging her arms in the air. "If you do that, you'll miss all the important things! What about friends? What about your track meets? What about *dating?*"

Florence's eyes narrowed. "What *about* dating?"

"You haven't been happy in months, and I think I know why!" Felicity insisted. "You need a boyfriend to be happy! Like me!"

That was so patently ridiculous that Florence spun around and headed to the school's front entrance.

Felicity followed her, now sidetracked into her favorite topic. "Eeee, have I told you about me and Daniel lately?! We're so, so, so close, it's like we're just one person! I can't wait until he kisses me again. The first time was when they were taking pictures for that magazine!" She giggled wildly. "It was so romantic!"

Or he's just using you until your fame runs out, you dumbo, Florence thought sourly.

"And our dates are, like, the greatest ever," Felicity chattered eagerly. "We have one every single day. I told him that we have to. Yesterday I cheered him in a ball game, and tomorrow, we're going to see two action movies with a bunch of his friends!"

"Neither of which are things you like doing . . ."

Felicity leaned her head against her hands. "I like everything when he's with me, silly!"

"Even when he's cheating on you?"

"He is not!" Felicity gasped. "How could you say such a thing?!"

Florence shook her head and went out the door.

Felicity pursued her, angry and insistent. "He isn't!"

"Felicity," Florence said with exasperation, heading down the path away from the school, "I *saw* him out with another girl last week, and it's not the first time."

Felicity waved a hand carelessly. "Oh, he explained that to me. That was his sister."

"I'm sure. The week before that?"

"That was his cousin."

"The week before *that?*"

"His cousin's sister."

"He has a suspicious number of female relatives!!"

"Aw, don't be like that." Felicity looked hurt. "He's my boyfriend! I know he would never cheat."

"How well does he even *like* you, Felicity?" Florence demanded. "As far as I can tell, he only paid attention to you after you were famous. He even turned you down before that."

"That's just because he had to think about it," Felicity protested. "We belong together. We're the perfect match. I've known it ever since I met him!"

"Yes, but has *he* known about it ever since he met *you?*"

"That's not fair!" Felicity yelled. "All my other friends know how wonderful Daniel is! Why don't you?"

Florence's jaw clenched. She wasn't going to say, *Because I've had a boyfriend who betrayed me, and I recognize the signs!*

Even now, a year and a half later, the subject was too painful. He hadn't just been a cad, after all. He had been the son of their arch-nemesis, a minion who was actively trying to kill them.

"Which reminds me!" Felicity burst out, her eyes lighting up. "I want to set you up with somebody! Daniel has this friend that —"

"Oh, *please,* no," Florence cut in.

Felicity looked uncharacteristically serious. "I'm worried about you, Florence! Just because your last boyfriend turned out to be a Deathwave doesn't mean you should give up on love completely!"

Florence winced.

"I know what you're doing," Felicity accused. "You're pushing everybody away. You turned down both the boys who asked you to the spring dance, and one of them was super cute and on the track team. You used to talk about boys with me all the time, but you haven't talked about a single crush since —"

"Felicity . . . drop it," Florence said wearily. "Okay?"

Felicity opened her mouth to apparently do no such thing, but then a figure leapt down from a tree beside them and landed in a menacing pose.

"Hi, Florence," Kendra announced. Her hair swished down behind her in a blonde waterfall. "Hi, Felicity."

"*Gasp!*" Felicity cried, instead of actually gasping. "It's Dark Kendra!!"

Kendra just stood up from her pose and glowered.

"It's Dark Kendra!" Felicity fretted, spinning one way and the other. "Oh, nooooo! It's Dark Kendra! She's finally attacking us! We're going to die!"

Kendra stared at her in stony silence.

"It's terrible!" Felicity wailed, putting her arm to her forehead. "Dark Kendra's here to attack us! She's going to kill us! We don't even have magic to turn her back from being brainwashed!"

Kendra's stony expression didn't change.

"Where's Daniel?" Felicity cried hopefully. "He'll protect me! And then his friend David can protect Florence, and they'll fall in love and live happily ever after! Where's Daniel? He'll protect me from Dark Kendra, right? Dark Kendra —"

"Stop calling me that," Kendra broke in, looking impatient. "It sounds stupid."

"Um . . . Kendra . . ." Florence said, finally finding her voice. "About why you're here . . ."

"Dark Angel?" Felicity asked.

"Way too generic," Kendra snorted.

"Dark Creamy?"

"What am I, a dairy product?"

"Dark Cream Angel?"

"Now, *that's* just *lame*."

Okay, Florence was no longer too surprised to be sarcastic.

"You know, Kendra," she said sardonically, pointing over her shoulder, "if you'd like to turn yourself in, the police station is that way."

"I know where it is, thanks," Kendra snorted. They had once volunteered there as police aides. "Look, we need to talk. I read something about you in a newspaper the other day —"

"You mean the announcement?" Florence cut in. "That was this morning."

"Dark Not-Angel? Dark Feathers? Dark Pretty? Dark Evil? Dark Justice? Dark Spiky?" Felicity pondered in the background.

"Okay, nine hours ago," Kendra said impatiently. "I slept on it while I was waiting for you to be awake. We need to talk about —"

"Not so fast," Florence shot back. "If you're here to talk, there are some things you have to do beforehand. *First,* you're going to say hello to your parents. *Then* you're going to apologize to them for just taking off without an explanation. After *that,* there is this thing called 'contact information' that you're going to give them. It may be a foreign concept to you, but the basic gist is . . ."

"Ha ha, very funny." Kendra folded her arms. "I'm here to see you, not them."

"I'm not joking!" Florence snapped. "It's been nine months, and you haven't gone back to see them once! Why would you think that's okay?! Clearly it wouldn't be hard for you to drop by once in awhile, since you're teleporting all over the world to random places! What was with that Chinchilla Fluffhair thing, anyway?"

Kendra sighed exaggeratedly. "Like I told the oracle, I had no way of knowing she was going to dive in front of my halo —"

"Is that your excuse for all the magical girls you've killed?"

"No, most of them deserved it."

"What about Dubai?" Florence demanded. "You broke the focus item of the only person who could control sandstorms just before a giant one hit the city!"

"Because she would have made it worse —"

"And Rouen! You randomly attacked a bunch of children!"

"One of them was a bully —"

"And Australia! Why were you aiding and abetting a mascot criminal?"

"Greased Lightning said that?" Kendra said incredulously. "What a liar! *She* was the one who was aiding and abetting —"

Felicity was still murmuring in the background. "Dark Sandals? Dark Halo? Dark Fluffywings?"

"Forgive me if I trust the word of a magical girl over a v—" Florence paused. "Dark *Fluffywings?*"

"Okay, that does it. Let's gag Felicity."

Felicity didn't seem to notice the threat. "Dark Black Outfit? Dark Cutesy?"

"Okay, look," Florence said, putting her hands on her hips. "You gave me an explanation before, and I thought it was nuts, but I still appreciated it. Now you owe your parents the same thing. Your dad was a former minion. He'll understand."

A hint of pain crossed Kendra's face. "I can't see them."

"Why not?" Florence demanded.

"Because I —" Kendra bit her lip.

Florence waited, folding her arms.

Kendra threw her shoulders back, and her eyes hardened. "I'm a *villain*, Florence," she said scornfully. "Villains don't lean on their parents. Besides, *you're* the one who's putting the world in jeopardy."

Florence's mouth gaped open at that blatant falsehood. *"Excuse me?!"*

"The Magical . . . Girl . . . Union," Kendra said triumphantly, punctuating each word with a jab of the finger. "Ever hear of it?"

"Of course I have!" Florence sputtered. "I organized it!"

"Um . . . guys?" Felicity put in hesitantly. "I think someone who was trying to cut school just recognized Kendra and ran back to the school to call the police . . ."

"Good!" Florence said, looking over at her. "Kendra's parents can visit her in jail."

"It's not like any cops can catch me. I'll just teleport out." Kendra shrugged. "But first, you need to listen to me."

"About what?" Florence asked with annoyance.

"About the Magical Girl Union."

"You mean the organization that I founded to protect the world from people like you?"

"I mean the organization that'll do just the opposite."

"What?" Florence snorted. "Don't be ridiculous."

"I live with someone who can see the future."

"What does that have to do with anything?" Florence demanded. "The Union is a *good* thing! Not to mention *you're* the one who used to joke that the world needed something just like —"

". . . I know I did," Kendra said quietly. "I thought it was a good thing, too. That's kind of my point."

"Well, then you know how impor—!"

"*I* would have founded the Magical Girl Union in my future, Florence!" Kendra snapped, pointing at herself fiercely. "I would have used it to take over the world and slaughtered anyone who didn't agree with me. That's why I defected to villainy — to stop the Union from ever happening in the first place!"

It felt like the world was tilting onto its side. "Wh-what?"

"Crimson Dragon," Kendra said. "Red blouse, long skirt with shredded layers. That's who you were in the future. You were my second-in-command, and you weren't capable of stopping me, or anyone else in the Union, for that matter."

Florence's breath quickened. "Crimson Dragon" was the name she'd almost given to the next power-up of her magical girl form. She'd come up with that name on the spur of the moment. She'd certainly never mentioned it to Kendra.

"Th-that's . . ." she stammered.

"Namikaze Tateru," Kendra said relentlessly. "Defector from the *kamikaze*. She was in my version of the Union. I'm guessing she's in yours, too."

Florence swallowed. "That's not a secret —"

"Dulcina Caramelo. I saw her on a battlefield I sent her into."

"She's a headliner in every press release —"

"Delicate Frost Princess! She's not mentioned in any articles, and she was arguing with me over something in that future. Is she in your Union?"

Florence's mouth went dry. That was a friend of Snowbelle's who had just barely joined.

"You probably have all the same people," Kendra said in an ominous tone. "Which means it doesn't matter whether it's you or me who leads them. They're going to do the same things."

Florence's mind jumped to Dulcina, whose persistent attempts to change the wording of the programs for the opening ceremonies to include lines about magical girl superiority had been incessant and irritating.

The Confrontation

Kendra abruptly raised her hand and held it out. "I once asked you if you'd trust me. If you'd join me. I'm asking again."

Florence's voice wouldn't work. She swallowed, then forced herself to speak. "I'm not going to be a villain, Kendra."

"I'm not asking you to. I'm asking you to come and see your future, to make sure you don't become one by accident."

Silence stretched between them. It was punctuated only by a siren in the distance.

"You should go with her," Felicity said. "Find out when me and Daniel are going to get married."

Florence sputtered with hysterical laughter. *Really, Felicity? Really?*

Kendra smirked. "All right. We'll ask. And in return, you'll tell the police nothing about this conversation."

Felicity gave her a thumbs-up. "Leave it to me!"

"Good." Kendra looked over at Florence. "Are you ready?"

Her shoulders tensed. "To do what?"

"Come with me." Kendra held out her hand. "There's someone you need to meet."

www.ingramcontent.com/pod-product-compliance
Lightning Source LLC
Chambersburg PA
CBHW022044050726
47591CB00003B/938